Edited by Matthew Cash/Em Dehaney, Burdizzo Books

Published in Great Britain in 2018 by Matthew Cash, Burdizzo Books Walsall, UK

The
WASSAILERS
Em Dehaney
Illustrated by
Krzysztof Wroński
BOOKS

CONTENTS

FOREWORD
GRAHAM MASTERTON

It's both fascinating and disturbing how many traditional folk characters are supposed to bring festive cheer to seasonal celebrations and feast days, and yet have a darker side to them.

I wrote a short story myself about "Anti-Claus", based on legends I had read about a winter holiday figure who would appear jovial and generous, but who would mete out a terrible punishment to anybody he thought had behaved badly during the year. He would know if you had been "naughty or nice" and if you had been "naughty" then he would rip the tiles off your roof and steal your children while you slept, and behead them.

Then there's Jack-in-the-Green, a tall spooky figure dressed entirely in leaves who appears in several spring festivals in the English countryside. He is supposed to have captured the spirit of summer, and the only way to release that spirit and ensure a good harvest is to rip him apart and burn him. You have to catch him first, though, and before you can do that he can break into your house and create havoc.

So it is with wassailers, who go from house to house at Christmas singing carols and expecting gifts or food or drink in return. Before 1752, when we changed to the Gregorian calendar, they would come around on "Old Twelvey Night", or January 17.

They sound innocent enough - the word "wassail" is an Old English phrase meaning "be in good health." But in days gone by the wassailers would be gangs of farm workers and ruffians who would go around drunkenly demanding money. They would protest that they were not everyday beggars, but if anybody refused to give them what they wanted they would burst into their homes and wreck them, and assault them too, sometimes fatally.

Em Dehaney's wonderfully creepy poem about wassailers brings that terror vividly to life. You can read it at any time of the year, but you should bring it out on Christmas Eve, when the carolsingers are coming around you neighbourhood, and think seriously if you want to open your door to them.

You never know. They might want very much more from you than coins or sweets.

Em's poem is accompanied by some striking illustrations by Krzysztof Wronski. All I can say about those is: "Upewnij się, że książka została zamknięta po zakończeniu czytania. Nie chcesz, aby postacie na rysunkach uciekły."

In other words, close the book when you've finished reading it. You wouldn't want the characters in the drawings to escape!

FOREWORD
EM DEHANEY

This poem was given its initial airing as part of Burdizzo Books 12 Days of Christmas Anthology. It was the first thing I had ever had published. When Matthew Cash decided to take a punt on a nobody he had never heard of, he told me the poem was like "a beautiful signature made of piss in the snow" (or similar, I may be paraphrasing, sorry Matty). We have since become partners in Burdizzo Books, and have grown our little Burdizzo Family of authors, fans and friends together. I'm immensely proud of what we have achieved so far, and everything we release just gets better and better (in my humble opinion!). This illustrated poem book has been a dream of ours since 2016, and when we got artist Krzysztof Wronski on board, he truly breathed life into our festive nightmares. As you will see, he is an astounding talent, and his pen and ink drawings create the perfect frame for my words. Thank you Kris for being so easy to collaborate with and your inspired take on the characters from my poem.

Huge thank you to Graham Masterton for providing the opening words to this book. I have been a rabid fan of his ever since I first read Prey as a 12 year old and got so scared I had to call for my mum in the night because I thought Brown Jenkin was coming to snatch me from my bed. He is a true great in the horror world, and a thoroughly lovely chap to boot!

Thank you to all the Burdizzo Family for supporting Matty-Bob and I, you really are a wonderful bunch of freaks and we love you all to bits. Tiny, bloody, meaty bits.

And finally, thank you to Matty, for being the first to recognise my genius (lol), for bringing me on board as editor at Burdizzo, for being my mate and for eating more scampi than I had ever thought humanly possible.

I hope you enjoy this book, dear reader, and heed its warning.

And if you hear a knocking
On a cruel black Christmas night,
Give well to the Wassailers
To stay warm and safe and light.

Em Dehaney, September 2018

On a moonshadow wintry night,

When the sky is a lake of black ink

Afloat with the bloom of the dying light,

The Wassailers will come to drink.

They may bang on your gate or your gantry,

They may tippity-tap at your wall,

They may ring on the bell in your pantry

But upon you they will come to call.

And sing.

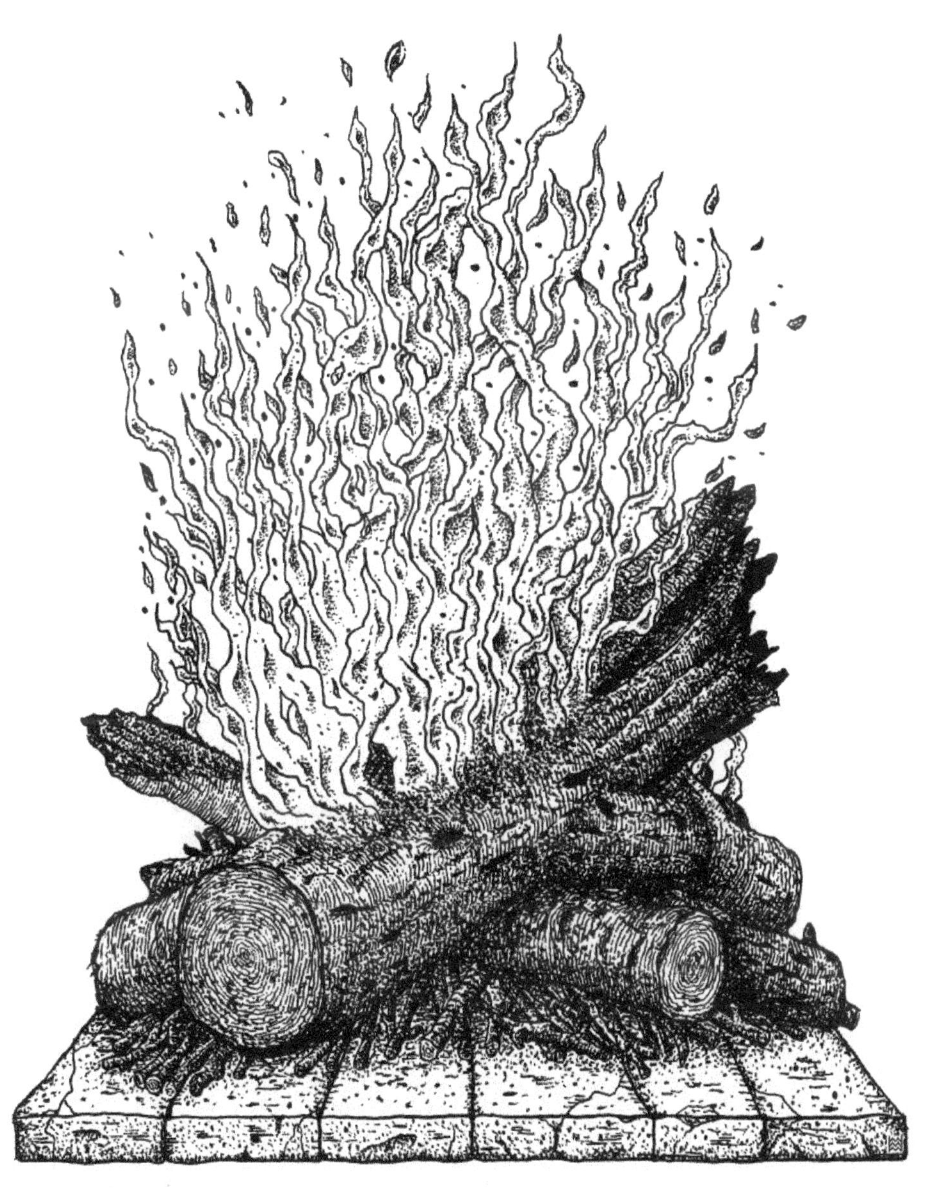

Sing of the forest a-withering,

Sing of the dark days ahead,

Of their prayers for a bountiful springtime,

Of their hunger for mead and for bread.

You may say, 'Come in and be warmed

By my yule log and sup on my beer.'

They will lay upon you a blessing

For a happy and healthy New Year.

You may tell them, 'Begone!

My family are poor,

My children are hungry and cry.'

The Wassailers will leave you be.

But beware,

If they find you are telling a lie.

If they see your table a-groan

With the fats of the summer and gin

And your pockets a-bursting with silver and gold,

The Wassailers will let themselves in.

They don't want your money or mutton

They eat meat of a different kind.

A game they will play

If you turn them away,

So keep what I tell you in mind.

Here they come a-wassailing
Among the leaves so green
Here they come a-wand'ring
The fairest to be seen

The Wassailers are four

And what games do they play?

First is Old Mother Tiptree, Broad of the May.

No virgin she, in her dress of red

With a crown of holly

And bay leaves round her head.

Master of the house,

Are you not entranced

By the way her rounded end sways?

Her bosom is swollen,

her lips are plump,

Full setting your loins ablaze.

You picture your manhood buried

In the fleshy wet mound of her cunt,

She tips you a wink,

To pour her a drink

And she laughs in your face with a grunt.

She will hold up her cup for you
To fill with your best barley beer.
When the goblet is drained
Does she let fly a belch,
And powder and rouge disappear.
Her chin now bristles with stubble.
That firm arse, so fulsome and thick,
Has become just a sack of grain
Tied around her waist,
Teeming with weevils and ticks.

O Master, she lifts up her skirts,

Presenting her monstrous snake.

The Mother gives life in the death of the Winter.

And, O man of the house, you will take.

Here they come a-wassailing
To take what you can't give
Here they come a-wand'ring
So pray that you might live

Do you like their game yet, Master?

The Wassailers have barely begun.

After The Mother has left you a ruin,

She beckons forth The Son.

This Wren-boy, this Knave,

Little Johnny Jack

Covers up his face with an old cloth-sack.

He is not a beggar or a singer or a thief

A sick and silent dumb-child

Hiding underneath.

What is in that box, boy?

What is in his box, indeed.

A tiny makeshift coffin

Dragging through the weeds.

You could guess it as a wren bird,

So small and cold and dead,

With its beak pointing upwards

And maggots in its head.

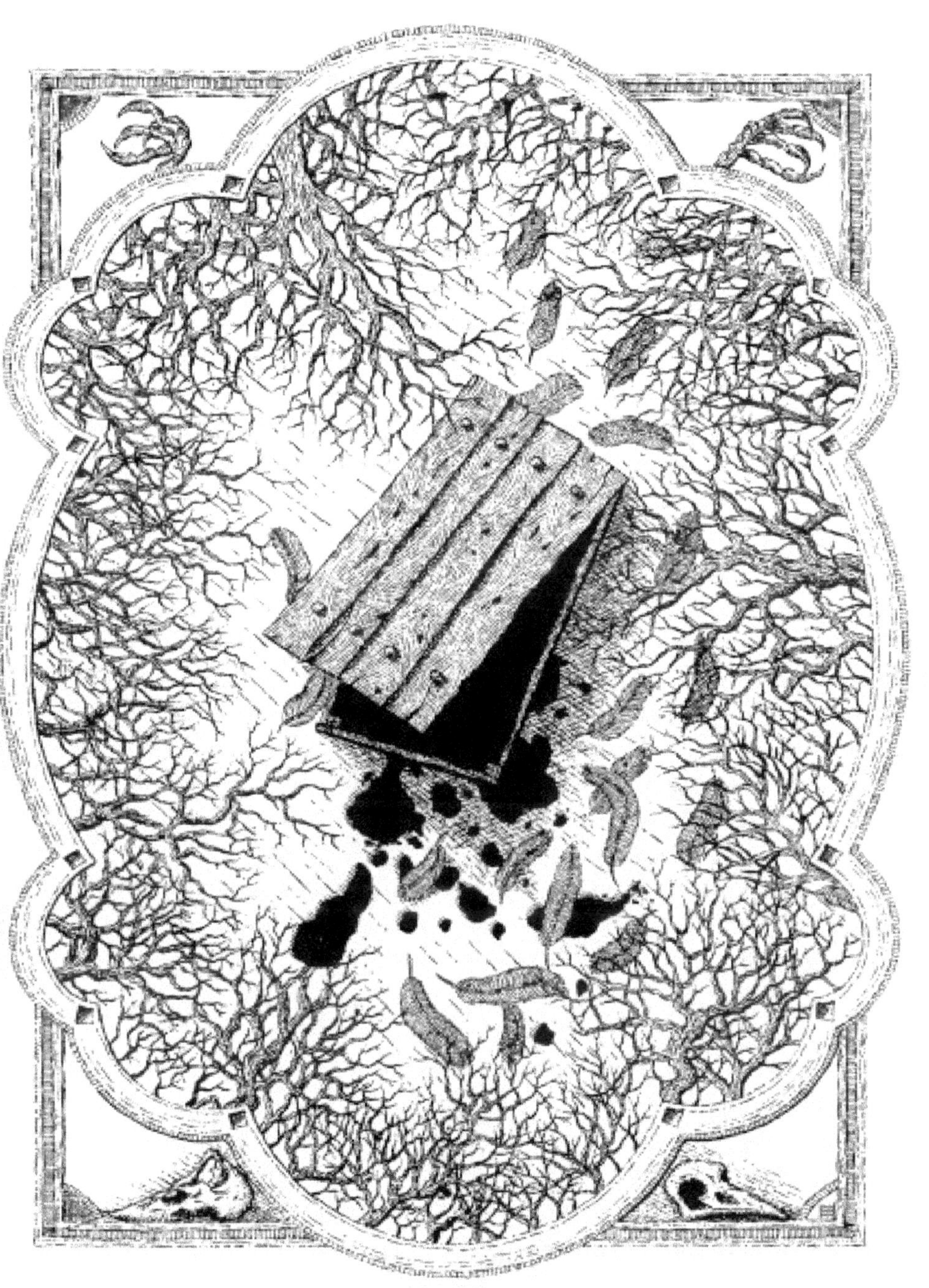

You could guess it as a robin,

With its feathers ruby red.

You could guess it as a swan, a goose,

A partridge or a hen.

You can guess it as you like,

You will ever guess it wrong,

For Little Johnny Jack sings only one song.

You must pay the price
For turning him away
As his tongue was cut out
When Johnny was a babe.
A penny or a tuppence
Would have done you no harm,
Now Little Boy Johnny takes
Your firstborn for his charm.

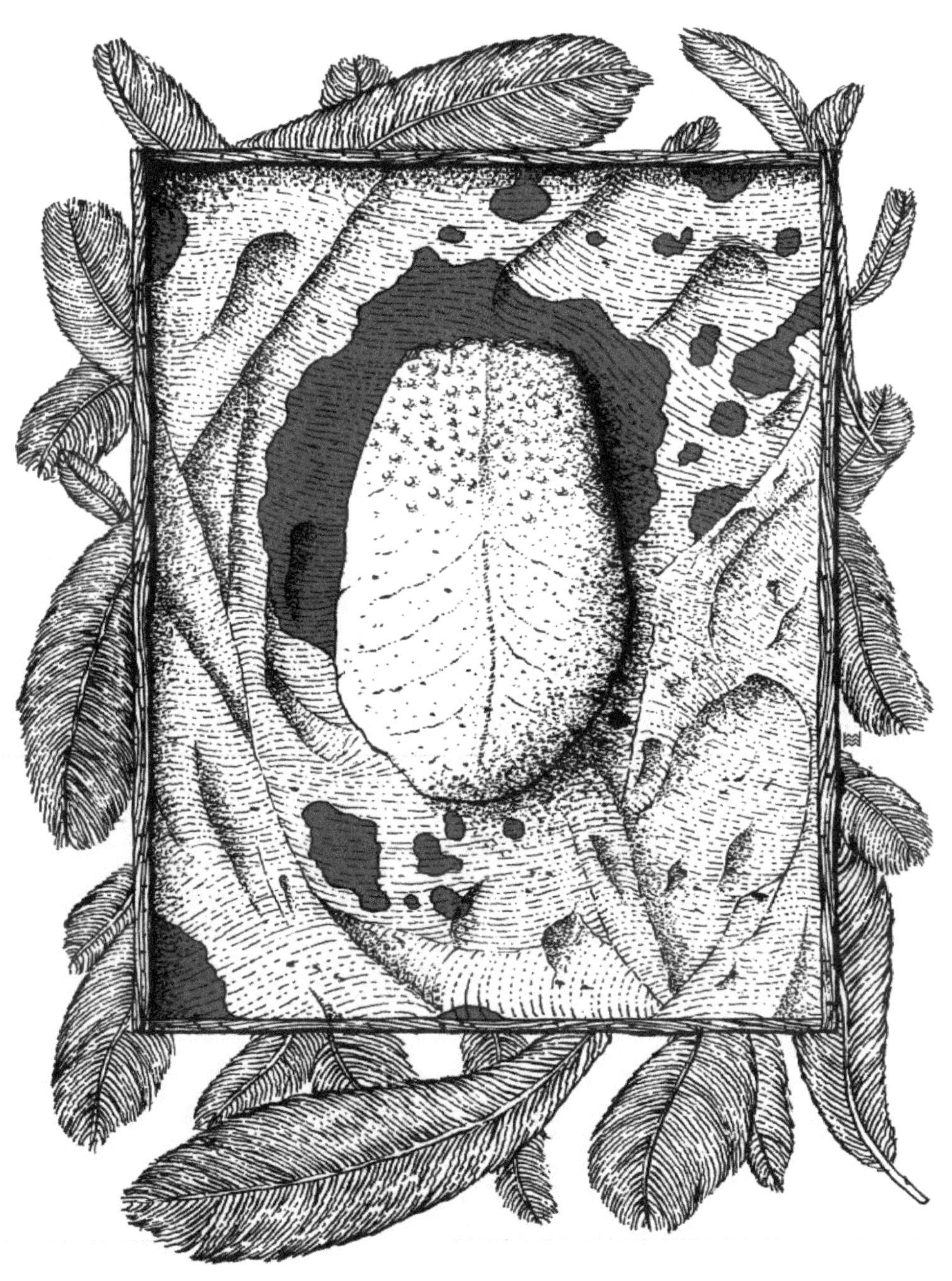

O Master of the house, listen to him crow

As he opens up the coffin lid.

His bloody tongue on satin,

Red roses in the snow.

New shoots devouring corpses of leaves,

A foundling child raised

By whores and grub-thieves.

Here they come a-wassailing
You will not hear them come
Here they come
A-wand'ring
Too fast for you to run

Who will step forward as number three?

O Master! O Mistress!

Just wait ‘til you see.

The Slicker, The Cutter,

The Butcher, The Flayer,

The Skinner, The Tanner,

The Stitcher, The Slayer.

Only one man but the size of two,

His great-helm is hewn

Of white maple and yew.

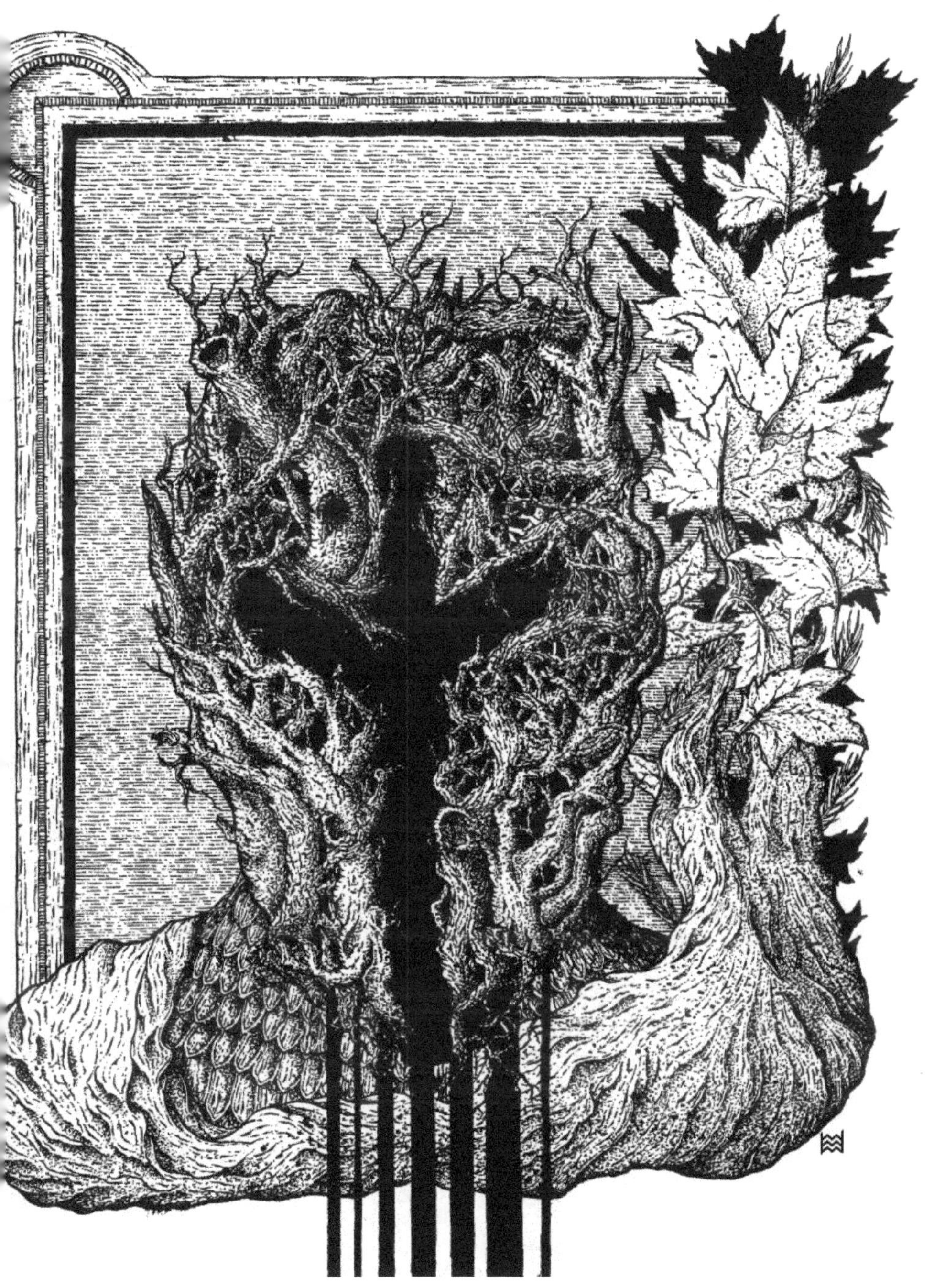

A vacant blank space where the visage should be,

He is faceless and dreamless

With no eyes to see.

No eyes to see that which he cuts

No ears to hear the ripping of guts

No nose to smell the piss and the lime

Only a mouth for singing in time.

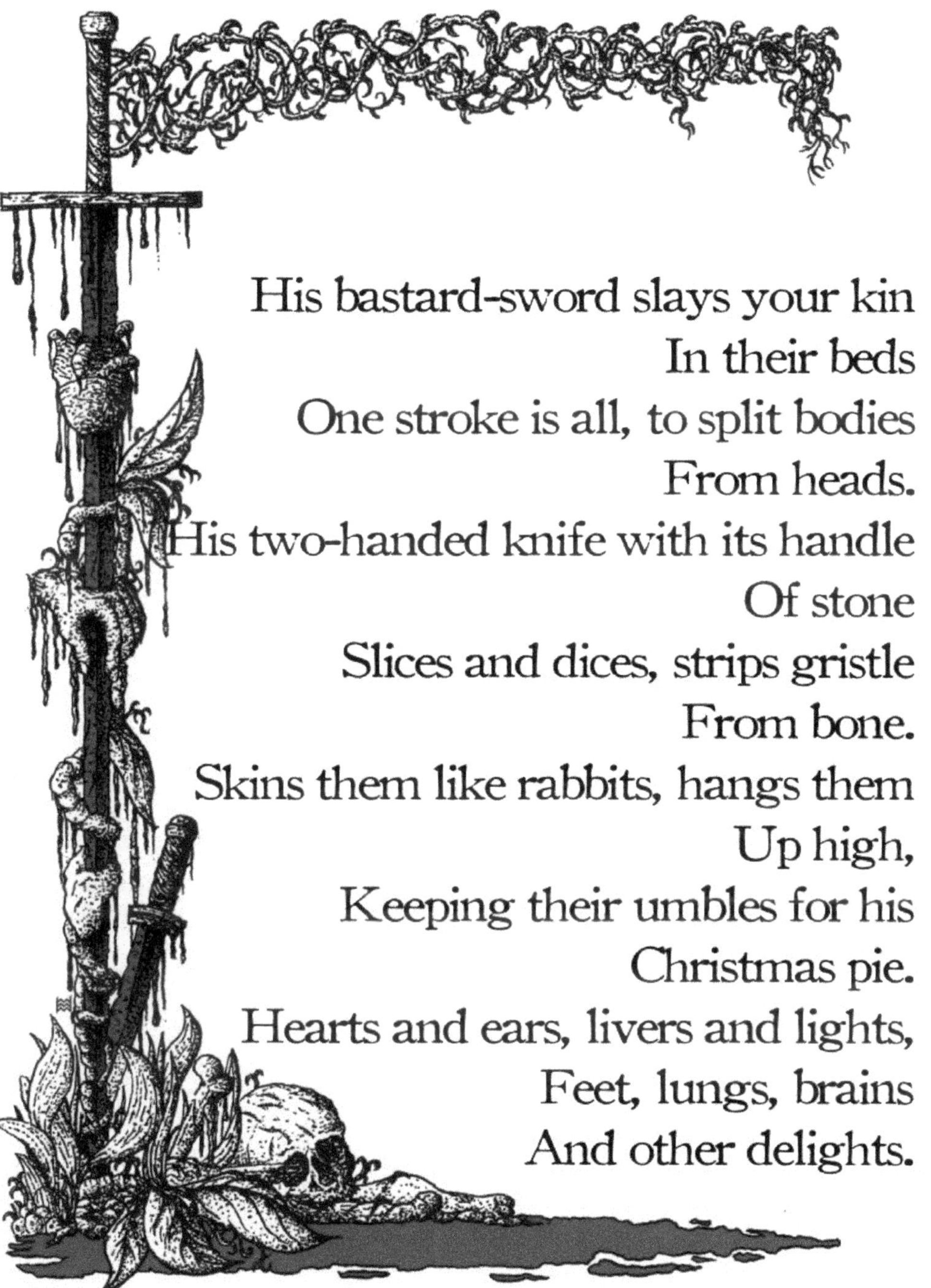

His bastard-sword slays your kin
In their beds
One stroke is all, to split bodies
From heads.
His two-handed knife with its handle
Of stone
Slices and dices, strips gristle
From bone.
Skins them like rabbits, hangs them
Up high,
Keeping their umbles for his
Christmas pie.
Hearts and ears, livers and lights,
Feet, lungs, brains
And other delights.

Here they come
A-wassailing
So tell them your sins
And don't lie
Here they come
A-belsnicking
Winter's a good
Time to die

And now for the last

The Apple Tree Man.

A nightmare creation,

Not part of God's plan.

His face is painted sable,

Horns grow from his brow,

He reeks of sweaty stable,

Of asses, ram and cow.

His feet are filthy hooves,
A string of teeth hang round his throat,
Breath like rotten fruit,
A matted winter coat.
He has a little purse,
Made of stretching leather skin.
Golden coins come out of it,
But ne'er a coin goes in.

His game; a simple wager,

He lays down a single bet.

Winner takes all,

The loser must die,

And he hasn't lost a game yet.

All you must do, O Master,

Guess the true name of your foe,

But I'll tell you a secret,

Now listen in close;

There isn't a true name to know.

The Apple Tree Man is older than names
As old as the soil and the seeds,
He cares not for flesh or for coin,
It is on fear that he feeds.
A suffering soul is the sweetest of treats,
And now Apple Tree Man has plenty to eat.
He stripes you with his switch,
You cry out for God, your saviour,
But the time for mercy sat with you,
When you turned away a Wassailer.

So good Master and good Mistress,

While you're sitting by the fire,

Pray think of those poor children

Who are wandering in the mire.

And if you hear a knocking

On a cruel black Christmas night,

Give well to the Wassailers

To stay warm and safe and light.

AFTERWORD
EM DEHANEY

If you feel inspired by the moral of my little Christmas poem (give well to charity or someone will come to your house in the dead of night, bum-rape you and eat your children… or something…) and you feel compelled to give, here a few of my suggestions for great charities that would be grateful for your donations. Or give food to a local foodbank, donate to charity shops, buy from charity shops, help out in your community whenever you can (you don't have to donate money, you can donate your time instead).

Medecins Sans Frontieres

Medical aid where it's needed most. Independent. Neutral. Impartial. They send 84 percent of money raised to their medical projects. Just two percent is spent on administration and staff costs. The rest is reinvested in fundraising.

https://www.msf.org.uk

Syria Civil Defence (The White Helmets)

A volunteer force helping innocent civilians survive in the most dangerous place in the world. 204 White Helmets have been killed saving the lives of men, women and children trapped in civil war-torn in Syria. As well as saving lives the White Helmets deliver public services to nearly 7 million people, including reconnecting electrical cables, providing safety information to children and securing buildings.

https://www.whitehelmets.org/en

DEC

When an international disaster strikes, the Disasters Emergency Committee (DEC) ensures that a joint fundraising appeal between all the major aid agencies is launched quickly. Funds are then divided according to which charities are best-placed on the ground.

https://www.dec.org.uk/

Burdizzo Books have a few smaller charities that we donate to as well, through the sale of our charity anthologies. 100% of profit goes to the charities.

NAPAC

The National Association for People Abused in Childhood (NAPAC) is the UK's leading national charity offering support to adult survivors of all types of childhood abuse, including physical, sexual and emotional abuse and neglect.

https://napac.org.uk

You can support NAPAC by buying a copy of The Reverend Burdizzo's Hymnbook.

Resources For Autism

Providing practical services for children and adults with an autistic spectrum condition and for those who love and care for them. They have a team of trained, enthusiastic and kind staff and volunteers offering a wide range of support in London and the West Midlands.

https://resourcesforautism.org.uk/

You can support Resources for Autism by buying a copy of Sparks or Under The Weather.

The Cystic Fibrosis Trust

The Cystic Fibrosis Trust is the only UK charity dedicated to fighting for a life unlimited by cystic fibrosis for everyone affected by the condition. They campaign, fund research, support clinical trials and offer support to everyone affected by the condition.

https://www.cysticfibrosis.org.uk

You can support The Cystic Fibrosis Trust by buying a copy of 12 Days of Christmas 2016 or 12 Days of Christmas 2017.

Five Gold Rings
Em Dehaney

1

Francine was my first wife. She was young and I was impatient. I harried that girl day and night to marry me. Every time I saw her at the corner store, buying groceries for her folks, I'd shout, 'When you gon' marry me, Miss Francine?'

She would just look down at the ground. But I could see her blushing, even through all them freckles. I turned up at the house one night, stood on that front porch with June-bugs flying all around, and I called for her Pa. I asked for her hand in marriage, all proper like. He had eight mouths to feed, not including him and his cold-fish of a wife, so one less under his roof would be a blessing. He didn't even ask Francine if she wanted to.

We married in the spring, full of innocence. Francine at least. I knew what I was doin'. The first time I shoved myself inside her she was dry and scared, and she tried buck me off like a mad little March mule. It never changed. I liked it that way. Her hair was so thin, it used to come away in my hands. I'll never forget the colour. Pale and clean as fresh bedsheets, and how it looked stained with blood like those same sheets on our wedding night.

I never meant for it to happen that way. It was all accidental. The baby. The fall down the stairs that left us childless and her barren at eighteen. Such a clumsy girl, that one. Even her Pa used to say it. Always walking into somethin' or droppin' the goddamn groceries. When I saw her lying there, all bent and crooked, a bloody mess, screaming and crying, I got as hard as ever had in my whole rotten life.

She was never the same after that. She didn't fight no more, just lay there, like a doll.

It was a sad day when she fell in front of that freight train.

2

Paulette was my second wife. I met her at the market, the handsome young widow. Everyone knew the story of my pale and crazy bride who took a leap in front of a train, stricken with grief. All the ladies in town got the soft eyes whenever I was around. There he goes, poor thing. I could look after him real good.

Boy, could that woman cook. I ate like a king when she was around. Coca-cola hams. Creamy mash potatoes and gravy. Peach cobbler. Buttermilk pancakes and candied bacon. I was fixin' to get fat as a stuck pig. My gut got so large I could barely see over it. She was a sturdy girl too. How her ass used to wobble when she ran away from me, how I could grab handfuls of overfilled sausage flesh when I finally caught up. I liked to bite into her, feel my teeth sliding through that buttery behind. She was meaty and creamy, like a fine steak.

I sure miss that Paulette. Shame she had such a smart mouth. Always running, like our old diesel genny. That genny needed a few good whacks with a wrench every now and again too, to keep it quiet.

Paulette don't run her mouth so much now it's fulla dirt and she's buried in the apple yard.

3

Lillie-May was my third wife. Met her at the roadhouse out on Breakneck Hill. She was a hellcat, that one. Thought she liked it rough. She had no idea. Daddy issues, that what they call it? Her Daddy was on his way to becoming a State Senator, had the money and the right connections. The only thing that stood in his way was that druggy dive-bar slut of a daughter. A career in politics means no skeletons in the closet. Or buried under the porch. Or wrapped in a blanket and rolled over a ravine.

Lillie-May loved to make her Daddy angry, to make him fret, and most of all, make him jealous. I saw the way his eyes lingered over her thighs when she wore them little shorts of hers. I could read his mind, picturing himself sliding a finger up inside them shorts, slipping it between her lips, then taking it out and getting a real good sniff of his daughter's delicious juices. And you what? I think she saw it too. And I think she liked it.

They found her hog-tied and branded, dumped by the side of the road after I skipped town. I never broke her neck, but that pretty little skull of hers was sure smashed in after I'd finished with it. I think I did her Daddy a favour, won him the sympathy votes.

4

Jackie was my fourth wife. Jackie, Jackie, O Jackie. Told her my name was Jack. Jack and Jackie, what a couple. Just like the Kennedys. I was new in town and she had a friendly face. She was one of them mousey types, you know the ones. Hair the colour they was born with, never wear a skirt over the knee, like helpin' the homeless and pretendin' they don't suck a dick. She said she had never met anyone like me before, I told her the same. I wasn't lying. I had never met a thirty year old woman who hadn't gotten drunk. I had never met a thirty year old woman who still had stuffed animals on her bed. I had never met a thirty year old woman who was savin' herself for the right man. I fixed all that in one goddamned night. Proposed to her over a cheap Mexican dinner and told her the cocktails were virgin, just like her. Took her tipsy ass home, dumped her on the bed and played stuff the animals 'til morning. She threw 'em all out soon after. Reckoned they smelled funny.

She used to talk about startin' a family, all her friends were expecting. Her friends thought I was cute. She did too, 'til I ripped her wedding dress. Fixin' to pack her things and go back to her mother that very night, she was. I took the lace veil from her hair, tied it round her neck and twisted 'til her eyes popped. O Jackie, you weren't expecting that.

5

Jack was my first husband. I knew that wasn't his name, just like mine wasn't Sally. Everyone has their secrets. We played house for a while, as the thunder clouds rolled. Oh, he had a cruel way and a dark eye, but he was handsome as The Devil. He said I was his one and only, and I believed him 'til the day I found four gold bands hidden in a beat up old tobacco tin in his top drawer. One of the rings had a wisp of hair tied round it. The blood stain had long since turned from red to brown, but I knew it was blood all the same. I put those rings back where I found 'em and made believe like they weren't there. 'Til the first time he whipped me so hard with his belt that my back split in two. Then all I could think about was those four gold rings, and how I was as sure as goddamn not gonna be number five.

I was a good girl. I waited and watched. I listened and learned. Sure, I got a few bruises, but it was worth it. The time had to be right.

Jack was my only husband. I took a straight razor to his throat while he slept off a rotgut hangover, slicing through turkey-neck and vocal chords. And when he opened his eyes in shock, putting his hands up to stem the gushing blood, I took that razor downtown and cut off the only thing he ever really loved. His gurgles and spurts filled the air like wedding bells as I threaded five gold rings on his limp and bloodied dick, and threw it out the window.

'Til death do you part.

Bonus Christmas inspired Burdizzo books stories which feature in

12Days: STOCKING FILLERS

12Days: 2016

12Days: 2017

All I Want For Christmas Is Ewe
Matthew Cash

"You're nothing but a fat, useless, stinking, fucking fat drunk." Daisy shrieked, her eyes squinting like they had the power to eject the same type of venom as her poisonous, puckered mouth. Her pristine blonde hair extensions fluttered in the breeze from the open doorway.

"Yer said fat twice," Eddie said, fingers laced over his belly and around his beer can. One thing he couldn't abide, lack of vocabulary, "obese, overweight, would 'ave been acceptable substitutes. Or if you wanted to go down the offensive route you could've said, 'you're nothing but a fat, useless, stinking, whale of a drunkard.'" Eddie paused and sipped his ale, "but no, you have to use small words and profanity, don't you?"

Daisy stared at the fat, useless, stinking, whale of a drunkard in disgust. His tattered white vest pulled down barely over his round belly, which was so big he used it as a fucking drinks stand. It was grotesque, the way it ballooned over the band of his tracksuit trousers. She couldn't believe she had married him.

Although fifteen years ago he had been a vibrant doting son, big and strong like only a busy farmhand could be.

But since his harridan of a mother kicked the bucket and the farm downsized, he did less and drank more.

Nothing phased or upset him, all he cared about was his pathetic farm which lost more than it made. She flicked her gaze over her shoulder to the red sports car, engine idling, behind her. Gordon, her lover, was everything he wasn't -good looking, rich, and good-looking, hell that was enough anyway. "I'm leaving you Edward, and you'll hear from my solicitor about divorce."

Eddie drained his can and tossed it over his shoulder before crossing his hands back over his belly, defiant. "I'm not agreeing to a divorce."

Daisy scowled at him maliciously, "I'm leaving you, I am in love with Gordon, I had sex with him in our bed."

"I know all that, I caught you remember?"

Yes, she did. And she expected a bit more of a fucking reaction when he had opened their bedroom door.

They had been in the throes of passion, Daisy straddling the younger, athletic Gordon in the position he referred to as 'the reverse cowgirl,' her back to him, hands resting on his well-toned abdomen, and she was cumming harder than she had ever done in her life. It had been amazing, then Eddie walked in, still in his filthy farm clothes, something she always berated him about, saw them and rolled his eyes. Actually rolled his eyes like she was doing something clichéd and typical.

"Ey," he had said in that horrific common accent of his, "yer could have at least worn some decent socks me old matey."

He had been referring to Gordon's socks, which were still on his feet, his left big toe pointing out towards the artex ceiling.

Eddie had then bent down beside their frozen, coital display, carefully moved their entangled underwear, and grabbed his tartan slippers. Almost like an afterthought he acknowledged her, "Don't forget to change the sheets afterwards, there's a love, not like last time, ey?" He then winked a piggy eye and went downstairs to sit in front of the television.

"Anyway," Eddie continued, drawing her from her flashback, "I ain't giving you a divorce, and I'll not ever sign no papers saying otherwise." All he had left was his mother's farmhouse and the animals, the place was slowly sinking into disrepair, he wouldn't let her have anything.

"Fine, well the solicitor will be in touch."

"Wait," Eddie called.

Finally, Daisy thought, now I'll get some kind of reaction. She looked at her husband quizzically.

"Merry Christmas," Eddie said warmly with a smile.

She span around and went out of the door, seething at her emotionless pig of a husband. Fuck Christmas and fuck him. It always amazed her at how bloody sentimental he was about Christmas time.

Daisy got in the passenger side of the sports car, Gordon grinned awkwardly, but gorgeously, "Alright?"

"Of course I'm not bloody alright." Daisy shrieked at him making him cower behind the steering wheel like a frightened child.

Gordon drove off, the twin beams of the car's headlights cutting swathes through the darkness over the farm that Daisy had paid absolutely no attention to.

"Merry, fucking, Christmas," she muttered scornfully out the window towards the small farmhouse.

Eddie moved his considerable bulk across to the kitchen and upped the temperature on the thermostat, it was a cold one this year. He pulled another can of ale from a crate that sat on the kitchen worktop and slumped back into the chunky, threadbare armchair that sat between kitchen and dining room. The Christmas decorations that hung all over the house were gaudy and ancient but Eddie loved them. They had been his mother's, as had the farm. He sighed, he missed his mother, she has been a good woman, not like Daisy. The inheritance money had nearly dried up, the farm didn't make much money either. Over the five years since she passed he had sold off a few of the animals and most of the land. Some of the animals he couldn't part with though, and the thought of using them for meat was a no go. Eddie had been a strict vegetarian since a child and when he learned where meat came from. He loved animals, they were better than people, more understanding and less judgemental.

The only money that came in was from the goats and dairy cows, of which he only had two left, Monica and Phoebe. Rachel had gotten ill last winter and never made it to the New Year.

Eddie raised his can in a toast to the empty kitchen and the memory of two lost beloved ladies, “to mother and Rachel."

The chickens brought money in from the free range eggs, and old Chandler the stallion was always popular with the local kids who wanted riding lessons, but the money was a pittance, as his mother used to say.

Daisy had wanted to turn the farm into a bed and breakfast, get rid of the stinking animals, convert the barn into a Swiss chalet. A Swiss bloody chalet. Oh how he had laughed at that. She hadn't cared for the animals anyway, saw them only as money makers. She wanted him to get rid of the pigs if he wasn't prepared to sell them for meat, and the money he got for Jemima's wool wasn't worth the effort.

Jemima was the last survivor of a whole herd of sheep and Eddie loved her. She had been known simply as number 69 to everyone but him, due to the number she had sprayed onto her side. But disease had struck the flock and all but her had perished. She was old, blind in one eye but he loved her.

Any animal that doesn't make money needs to go, Daisy said. Even the duck pond. She wanted that filled in, the 'useless' birds slaughtered and the land to be used for something more bountiful.

Eddie sighed and pulled his jumper on. It hadn't been what he has hope for, marriage. Whilst they nursed his dying mother he planned to turn the farm into one of them family places where the parents could bring the kiddies and show them the animals. Teach them all about the history of farming and agriculture. He would give them the tour, teach them how to care for the animals, lambing season would be popular too. Springtime was great on farms, All that new life, cute baby animals bouncing about the place.

It would have been great.

Eddie wiped a tear from his eyes when he wondered how he was going to pay for the shipment of feed and bedding that he desperately needed to order for the animals. It really was getting colder now, and his bank account would not be sufficient. On the day before Christmas Eve he found out she had withdrawn almost everything from the bank. Daisy had bled him dry. All he had was his animals, what he referred to his furry family.

The days rolled on and whilst Daisy was whisked away somewhere sunny for sand, sea and sixty-nines, Eddie was trying to cope with fast diminishing temperatures and livestock who were almost out of food or hay. He wasn't too bothered about himself, the bills were always paid a few months in advance and he had enough food to last him for ages. But he wondered how he would look after his animals.

Outside was a winterland of Arctic proportions, the ground rock hard with a frost that never lifted, the ducks skidded around on their frozen pond, the cows relied on whatever feed Eddie could give them. The sun had fucked off and done one big time, and the clouds above bulged with the threat of a never-ending blizzard.

Eddie studied the weather and knew that this was going to be the harshest of winters he had ever experienced in his fifty years. As he sat surveying his land, supping at a flagon of his father's moonshine he had dredged up from the cellar, a blazing star twinkled briefly between the swollen bastard snow clouds. Like the star over Bethlehem filled the shepherds of millennia past with awe and wonder this celestial body ignited something within Eddie as he lolled in the Eddie-shaped mould of his armchair. He opened his mouth and lifted his right buttock and simultaneously burped and farted. Then jumped straight up and out of the chair as something extraordinary happened.

A bright, blazing blue beam, as bright as the sun, seemingly shot down from the star parting the snow clouds.

Eddie pressed his face against the cold glass of his window and watched with transfixed with delirious ecstasy as a figure, glowing blue from the light, floated down to the farmyard.

A spectral cow, he could tell it was Rachel by her markings, beautifully washed and preened hovered upright outside his kitchen window. Her forelegs paddled the air in front of her whilst the rear stood still above the frozen ground. She was lit with an ethereal luminescence, her eyes sparkled with blue love and affection. A blinding disc of white hovered like a planetary ring around and above her head, and glowed with the same inner light as the massive white wings that spread around her.

Tears of complete joy fell down Eddie's face, he fumbled with the back door lock and ran out into the yard to greet his angelic cow. All around him in the now lit farmyard he could hear his animals becoming excited, the lowing of Monica and Phoebe the cows, the neighing of Chandler the horse, the snuffles from the pigs, Jemima's distinctive bleat and the various quacks and clucks from the ducks and chickens. They sang out their animal hosanna for the return of their lost friend Rachel.

Eddie fell to his knees on the soft snow and hard mud, gazing up in religious ecstasy at the floating cow who had spun in the air to face him. Her bulging udders pulsated at eye level, the teats waving this way and that like she was under water.

A voice came from her wide mouth, her big thick tongue moving unnaturally to pronounce words and sounds not designed for one of her species. She sounded exactly as Eddie imagined, all animals had a voice in his mind, silken, creamy soft tones that enveloped him like warm chocolate. She told him, praised him, thanked him for all his good work, instructed him of what to do before he and her friends could join her in the pastures of Heaven. Before she left him her udders burst and baptised him with thick, gluttonous cream, sparkling with heavenly gold light.

It took him all night, but he was relentless and unstoppable now he knew his mission in life. Rachel the cow angel had spoken to him, told him the way it would be. At first he wondered whether the ever-fermenting, decades old moonshine of his father's had addled his brains, and that the whole religious visitation had been concocted by whatever poison it had mutated into. But when he awoke, early on Christmas morning, covered in Rachel's thick colostrum, her womb filled with the calves she was unable to bear whilst alive, he knew it had been real.

Everything was white when he peered from his bedroom window, the blackened carcass of the burnt farmyard buildings jutted out of the snow like the spindly twig arms of a overturned snowman.

The barn where Chandler, Phoebe and Monica and the goats had resided had taken the longest to burn, the wood damp and cold with the recent weather. But when the fuel

Eddie had doused the remnants of the last haystacks started burning the wood soon dried out and went up.

He left the pigsty and chicken huts, they would be covered by the snowstorm by now anyway. The amount of snow that had fallen since Rachel's departure had been miraculous for one night's fall. Four feet, he estimated, and that had all been after he had destroyed his farm.

“Oh well," Eddie said to no one in particular, "best get ready for Christmas dinner."

Daisy swallowed her pride and got out of the taxi. She couldn't believe the last few weeks she had had. The holiday had been great, Gordon even greater, but he had been so dull. Dullness she could have put up with if it hadn't been for the bloody barmaid at the hotel they stayed in. She had caught them at it on a secluded part of the beach. She had taken ill with a migraine and left Gordon to go out alone. Afterwards, early evening, she took a stroll to clear her head and saw them fucking behind a sand dune.

And now she was back. There was no doubt that Eddie would have her back. Sure, she would have to eat humble pie for a few days, be the dutiful housewife, let have sex with her other than on his birthday, but he would have her back. And she had nowhere else. Yet. She would spend the next few weeks searching for somewhere new to live, she would persuade him somehow to sell up, sell the animals and the farm. Then she would take the money and scarper.

Daisy froze when she walked down the wet lane to the farm entrance, the melted snow had caused floods nearby but the ground was high up here. “What the fuck?" Their huge red barn was devastated, burnt out, laying on the ground like a upturned dead spider.

A fire.

Did they have insurance? She was certain that Eddie would have. A smile lit up her face, insurance would mean a pay out. Money. If somehow Eddie had been caught in the fire she would have his life insurance too. Suddenly her dreams of turning the land and buildings into a bed and breakfast were becoming realistic.

She could use the money to rebuild and set up business.

She passed the pigsty, chicken huts and run and saw that they were deserted.

Her blood ran cold, what if that robbing bastard had sold all the remaining animals and buggered off with all the money? It would surprise her, Eddie wasn't that sort of man.

She left the empty huts and turned to the farmhouse. It too seemed quiet, empty.

The door was locked, curtains drawn. Daisy rooted in her bag for her set of keys and entered the house.

The smell hit her straight away, a strong animal reek. Chickens waddled across the filthy carpet, pecking at morsels amidst the detritus. The kitchen was a mess, the cupboards raided, their doors hanging from busted hinges. The chickens congregated around a burst sack of economy cornflakes.

Something shifted in the half light, beside her in the lounge. "Jesus fucking Christ." She exclaimed as Chandler the horse snorted at her, lifted his tail and dropped great, big dollops of steaming shit on the rug. He moved casually to a hay bale that filled up the dining table.

Monica and Phoebe lay on the lounge carpet, the three piece suite was ruined, the plasma television covered with a dry translucent film of animal saliva.

A rustling and the scuffling of hooves tore her eyes away from the cows in the lounge, as two goats came trotting down the stairs, her best lingerie wrapped around their horns, half chewed. The black goat that Eddie called Ross gazed at her, his lower jaw going side to side as he chewed on her gusset. All around the walls and furniture had been gouged by horns or nibbled by teeth. Sodden paper Christmas decorations had turned into a soggy mulch on the floor where they soaked up animal urine.

A sudden waft of sweaty shit and rotten food came from the cellar door, the pigs had found the contents of the pantry, sacks of potatoes, dried fruit and pickles.

Quacking came from the downstairs bathroom, their four ducks taking it in turns to dive in and out of the overflowing bathtub.

Daisy whirled around and around, her home was ruined, everything was destroyed. A hollow groan escaped her throat at the madness, Eddie had obviously flipped his lid, her leaving him having a more serious effect than he had made out.

A thud from upstairs, and groans of pleasure. Daisy was struck by an unexpected bout of jealousy. He never made noises like that when we had sex. Eddie had always been a quiet lover, missionary, a few thrusts and a grab of one tit was generally all she got before his face screwed up like he had constipation and he came. Even when he came it felt as though it just oozed out unenthusiastically, rather than gushing like Old Faithful as Gordon had.

But as she climbed up the stairs, over the contents of her wardrobe, her best dresses ruined, she heard bed springs boinging and the headboard banging. The dirty old bastard was going at it like a demon possessed. But who the hell would he have up there?

Daisy reached out to touch the door handle, waiting for Eddie's panting to reach a crescendo. He had ruined epic sex for her and Gordon that time, she never did feel like she even came close to cumming as hard as she was when he had caught her at it. She would ruin his fun too.

She heard his breathing become more rapid, the headboard smashing against the wall, the bed sounding like it would explode at any point, his voice was raw and rough with lust when he growled out, "oh God yeah Jemima."

Daisy gasped and yanked open the door. But Jemima was what he called the...

Jemima baa'd at her as if to confirm her suspicion. The ewe stood on the bed, Eddie naked behind it, fingers digging deep into her greasy wool. Daisy stood slack-jawed, words failing her at the scene of perverse bestiality before her. She lowered her eyes and saw that Eddie still had his socks on, the heel of the right one was completely missing. After what he had said to Gordon this was the thing that tipped her over the edge. She stared at her sheep-shagging husband and pointed at his holey sock, "you fucking hypocritical cunt."

Eddie sheepishly pulled out of Jemima, the sheep bleated disappointedly and walked across the bed to chew on the pillow.

"You're crazy," Daisy said retching and shielding her eyes from Eddie's erection, "insane. You'll go to jail for this."

Maybe that would work in her favour, he would surely get a severe prison sentence for this, not only was it animal cruelty, but she was pretty sure having sexual relations with them too was a crime. She could let the bailiffs come and take everything they needed. Hell, they could bulldoze the place for all she cared. Whatever was left she would take and leave him for good. She looked at her emaciated husband, covered in his own, and God knew what else's filth. He'd even lost weight since she had left. Pitiful. With any luck he would miss his animals so much in jail that he would kill himself. Then she would get his life insurance too.

Eddie raised his head and grinned at her, his teeth caked with plaque, old food and what looked like wool. There was a sinister element to his expression, one she had never seen before. He reached out a doughy arm behind him and grabbed what appeared to be a wooden staff. Daisy recognised it as the ancient shepherd's crock that used to hang above the fireplace, his grandfather's.

Eddie pointed the curved end towards her, his voice dripped with an evil she would never think him capable of, “I am the Shepherd and this is my flock."

Daisy turned and bolted for the bedroom door, with Eddie's severe mental deterioration who knew what he was capable of. She made it to the top of the stairs when she felt the hook of the shepherd's crock loop round her ankle and caused her to trip. She bundled down the staircase and landed at the bottom in a heap. At the top of the stairs Eddie appeared, still naked, still erect, and laughed. To her amazement he began to sing as he descended the stairs. “whilst shepherds watched their flocks by night, all seated on the ground."

The fall had hurt her but she didn't think anything was broken, the crap on the stairs would have cushioned part of the fall.

He muttered something inaudible and her ribs were suddenly crushed by the front right hoof of Chandler. The weight of the horse shattered her ribcage and sent splinters of bone through her lungs instantly.

Chandler's other leg hovered above her face, frozen, waiting for the order from Eddie.

"An angel of the Lord came down," Eddie sung, arms spread out, joyous as he stood over his wife.

Daisy choked on her own blood whilst she fought for air that would not come.

"And glory shone around." Eddie said with a hint of sadness, then nodded to the horse. Chandler stomped his hoof down onto Daisy's head putting her out of her misery.

Eleven Pipers Piping
Matthew Cash

When I first saw the ad in the Daily Record I thought, "Fuck me, they desperate for an audience or what?"

The Edinburgh Royal Military Tattoo, the traditional annual extravaganza that sucked tourists from all corners of the world like a weathered old pisshead draining the glass for the last few dregs of cheap shitey lager.

Be proud of your country, that's what the advert said, like we weren't already. I fucking love Scotland me. I guess they wanted more of us natives going to one of thecountry's largest events rather than millions of people from around the world.

I usually just watch the show on the BBC whilst having a carry out and a bevvy. But this year I found myself filling out the wee competition form in the newspaper and sending it off. It was freepost and all.

Well, the days wound on and on, posters began to be slapped up everywhere advertising the Fringe festival which usually coincided with the Tattoo. Showmen from some of the more zany acts would cruise the Royal Mile in their fancy garb telling all and sundry to flock to their shows.

It was a good time of the year, I didn't mind the tourists, it brought some culture to the place, and last year I pulled a couple of yank lassies that came in my local so it wasn't too bad for me.

Anyways, I put it down to drink, drugs, too much cheese before bedtime, the usual suspects, but for a few weeks after filling out that wee form I started having weird dreams.

Now, I hadn't really been to the castle since I was a nipper. My dad took us just before he took himself off to England with some scuzzy yo-yo knickered floozy. But, being a resident of this fine city meant it was always up there looking down at us. The castle is bloody impressive, sitting up there scowling down at the city, acting the hard man up on its mountainous pedestal.

So even though I hadn't been up there since I was a laddie I was up there again in the first of these recurring dreams.

It was night time and I was standing at the walls next to one of them big cannon jobbies, the ones they use to fire at one o'clock each day. I was taking in the view of the city at night, the lights, the monument protruding like a space rocket out of a Giger painting, and it was fucking beautiful. That was when I heard bagpipes, not so strange I hear you say, being in Scotland's finest city and all, but it took me by surprise. It sounded funny, distorted like. I turned and wandered the grounds to find the source. It didn't take me long, I mean bagpipes aren't exactly your most inconspicuous musical instrument. The castle was deserted, something I thought odd. places like these should be secured twenty-four seven, but nonetheless I walked towards the source of the cacophony. As I got closer I could see the piper standing on one of the walls, his back to me, the pipes tucked under his left arm. I was impressed but not too surprised, Scotland the brave and all that, to see him standing up there without any safety harnesses or anything above what is probably a several hundred feet drop. I may have over or underestimated that measurement but I don't really care, I'm no mathematician. It was a long way down, enough to make you go from man to jam in under a minute.

I noticed there was something weird about him, fanning out behind the back of his head was a spray of something, a semi-transparent headdress, like when you see fashion models with stuff sticking out of their hair, feathers and shit.

Whether it was the moon poking out from behind a cloud or just some convenient dream coincidence, a dim glow illuminated his fucked up tiara. It was the whacking great glistening hole in the back of his head that gave it away. A headshot bullet wound in suspended animation. The spray at the back, shards of skull, matted clumps of hair, chunks of brain, blood splatter frozen like red jewels, crimson pearls, molten wax seals with a bullet's stamp. All the time he played the damn pipes oblivious to this, surely fatal, head wound. I recognised the tune. Scotland The Brave.

Obviously I'm a rational man, it was a trick, a marketing ploy for one of the festival acts, a costume. I leant against the wall and checked out his front. They had done a really good job, made him look like he'd been in a car crash or something. He was blackened and red. His fancy clothes melded to his skin, the front of his kilt had been burnt away and there was just a mess of gore from his chest downwards, he wore his entrails like a shrivelled tatty leather apron.

"Awesome costume brother," I shouted up at him. He ignored me, not even a wink, but then again he didn't look like he had any eyes. One was just a blood filled hole and the other a crisp black cavern.

It's weird, even though I could see no one other than the lone piper all around me, the deafening cries of thousands of people woke me from my dream.

Turns out it was my clock radio alarm playing some upbeat hip hop bullshit to get me the hell out of bed. I always made sure I tuned it into the most annoying radio station so as to piss me off enough to get me out of bed.

I punched the bastard, it was novelty pish, designed like a punchbag, and shuffled through to the kitchen. That was when I saw the letter on the mat.

I picked it up frowning like I'd never seen a bloody envelopebefore, and slit it open with my thumb. A posh embossed ticket to the Edinburgh Military Tattoo.

"Fuck me," I thought. I'd never won a thing in my whole life, even in sports at school the only thing I managed to catch was athletes foot in the changing rooms. I was stoked man, really stoked. There was nothing else in the envelope aside from a brief compliments card. It made me happy but I think I've already said that, so even though the date was still a few weeks away I went out after breakfast and bought myself a new shirt.

The big day came and I splashed out a bit on a few drams of quality whisky from one of the posher places on the Mile, I thought why not man, it wasn't every day people like me got to go anywhere nice.

I found a nice restaurant, had a blinding steak and chips, you could tell it was posh nosh, Gordon Blue or whatever the fuck it's called, because the dinner came on a chopping board and the chips had the skins on still. It was lush, especially with the whisky afterwards.

When I left the place I walked up the Mile and up Castle Hill towards, well, the castle. Hundreds of people were already flocking in that direction, groups from every corner of the globe, a hive of activity with the buzz of dozens of different languages. Made a change from the only person being unintelligible I came into contact with being Fred the jakey from outside the bookies, I can tell you. It was nice, different.

The seating in the Esplanade had undergone a big change a few years back but I couldn't tell the difference, looked the same as it did on the fucking telly only way bigger.

I was shown to my seat by some young spirited usher and just sat there taking in the experience.

Where I was sat was dead centre like, opposite the castle. Best seats in the house brother, not far from the front either.

I sat whilst the place filled up, probably maximum capacity, every seat seemed full. A bunch of female backpacker types were sat next to me, I'd didn't know where they were from, they weren't that talkative to me, even when I said "hello", but whatever, I wasn't going to let in shit in my shower if you know what I mean.

Finally the show started with hundreds of dancers from, I forget where they said now, Zimbabwe or somewhere, and they did this cool tribal piece with yelling and drums.

After that there were some wee lassie dancers from Skye and the islands up north, really beautiful man.

The New Zealand fellas, the Maori is it? The natives came on with all their gear and did one of them mad dances they do at the rugby. A haka. Scary bastards but purely belter too, I was close enough to see the wee veins in their heads pop up when they yelled.

Things started getting more traditional when the Scots Guard paraded with their brasses and pipes and tartan, that was more like it. They played a medley of all the greats. I hoped to Christ no one would try and be modern like that year they went and did that Gangnam Style dance, that had been fucking ridiculous.

At what I guessed was halfway through their set,, two almighty fucking crashes that sounded like the Devil farting came from each side of the arena and everything went white for a second.

I instinctively ducked into the footwell, as chaos surrounded me. My first thoughts were the obvious ones. And it turns out I wasn't wrong. Terrorists.

Panic everywhere, people were screaming and clambering over the seating to flee the castle grounds. I risked a peep over the seat in front of me and wish to God I hadn't.

The seating up each side of the arena had bloody great holes blown in them like an asteroid had shot through the place. Debris from the blasts was everywhere, crowds on the sides of the blast zones writhed like maggots to get away from the fires that were dotted about. There were pieces of people everywhere, all over the Esplanade. A lot of the performers had taken the worst of the blast but those lucky to survive it were busy trying help their fallen comrades. It was a battle zone.

Then I saw the lone piper, way up at the undamaged part near the main castle. A voice boomed over the speakers, those that hadn't been destroyed. "Keep calm and head towards the piper."

The fellow was limping badly, one of his legs was red and ruined, and no one was paying attention to him even though he waved his arms and shouted. So he took up the bagpipes and began to play them. This poor heroic fucker played wonderfully, it was in his blood this beautiful, beautiful bastard. He had been on fire for fuck sake and there he was playing, trying to round up people from every nation like some beautiful bloody ginger Scottish Jesus.

People had cottoned on and slowly but surely the frantic multitudes began moving in his direction.

That was when another threat presented itself.

From out of the crowds came the sound of rapid gunfire and more screaming.

People started rushing around and running back towards me. I spotted the gunman just before I threw myself back to the floor out of the way of trampling feet. Aside from generic t-shirt and jeans that was all I noticed about him.

More gunfire came from further down where the crowds were rushing from the piper back towards the main entrance.

I'm not a religious man, , but if this was for a holy cause then I would hate to meet the God that condoned this shit.

One of the young students who had been sat near me stood on the steps, looking for her friends. I yanked at her trouser leg for her to get down when a bullet whipped through the air, ruffled her hair and blew her brains out of her forehead. My scream was but a wank in the ocean compared to the hell-noise around me.

I hid, I cried, I feared for my stupid useless fucking life, as thousands of people were being mowed down by crazy bastards.

A break in gunfire.

That was when I heard the piper still playing, he was joined by others, a signal for people to still come their way, that together they would be stronger.

The gunfire recommenced and I thought of my miserable existence and the people being killed all around me. I belonged with them. I was nothing.

One of the gunmen was now stood right beside me, a black machine gun in his hands, bullets showering the running people ahead of him, smiling as he shouted something in another language.

I got the bottle of whisky stowed in my pocket, twisted the cap off and took a large swig. Might as well die with a belly full of whisky. Maybe the fumes on the breath of my dead body would mask the reek of piss in my pants.

Then something took over me and I found myself leaping up and smashing the cunt over the head with the half-filled bottle. He hadn't known what had hit him and the fear that he may get up again once he had fallen made me go a little bit crazy. I stomped on that fucker's head until there was nothing left.

I shook, I had not expected that, but a fighting part of me had been ignited, if I was going to be killed by one of these bastards I was sure going to try taking at least another one down first. I grabbed his gun and a spare magazine I saw protruding from his trouser pocket. I didn't know what the hell I was doing.

I crouched back down and peeked over the seats towards the gunfire. I made out at least three other gunmen at different positions, open firing on innocent people.

My heart was still rampant from beating the fella to death, I wasn't worried whether or not I'd be arrested. I doubted that I'd last the following ten minutes.

I crawled along the footwell behind the row of seats over handbags dropped in the melee. Every now and then I popped my head up to see what was happening down on the Esplanade. The crowds were rushing to a band of determined pipers and the surviving military men began to skirt around them fencing them in. They were trying to protect the people but all the marching ones had were empty decorative rifles with fixed bayonets. The gunmen cut a swathe through the people running towards what they thought was safety. I saw mothers, fathers, sisters, brothers, sons and daughters from all around the world being gunned down by these deluded heartless bastards.

A few other people, Japanese I think, had taken to hiding behind the seats like me and shrieked when they saw me crawling towards them with a bloody great gun. I motioned for them to stay put but they were just frightened. The father grabbed his wife and the two wee bairns and legged it down the steps away from me.

The gunman pacing this part of the arena swivelled his weapon towards them and I saw the two bairns' faces explode all over their parents before the spray of bullets obliterated their legs and they tumbled down onto the bodies of their dead children.

I ran at the bastard.

I've never fired a gun before, I mean I've played your video games and stuff but that's the most I've done. I wasn't expecting the kick it gave when I pointed it at the fucker and pulled the trigger. The thing buzzed in my hands and a series of red spots like blooming flowers dotted the man's white shirt and went up in the air as the force of the thing made me shake. I took my finger from the trigger and my arms felt numb.

I saw the other two signal towards me and one of them moved across the rows in my direction.

I continued towards the Esplanade with the intention of handing over the weapon to one of the soldiers, the brave bastards who were trying to keep the people safe. The bombs had blown great holes in the stands, debris was dropping off the sides, I think some were actually people jumping. I could hear sirens over the screaming and the whir of approaching helicopters. I hoped to hell they would hurry up.

The gunman fired at me and I dropped to the floor, the bullets missing me by inches as they zipped past my ears and made mincemeat of the padding in the seats. I stuck the gun over the back of a chair, aimed it in his general direction and fired it once more. I risked a look,hoping I had struck lucky. I hadn't, the fucker, and now he had seen I was armed, decided to spend the last of his time picking off the defenceless.

The gunmen worked their way towards the crowd of people in the centre of the Esplanade where the pipers still played, and the wounded were dragged amongst the debris from the bombs. The soldiers stood firm and defiant, but there wasn't that many of them to protect that number of people. I remember thinking that if only they would all rush the gunmen as a collective, they could take them down.

The gunmen laughed and shouted more gibberish as they stormed across the Esplanade, reloading from spare clips hidden about their clothing. A few of the brave soldiers did do as I had thought, a group of about four rushed towards the gunman nearest to them but the bastard cut them down in a heartbeat.

I had lost all self-concern then, I just ran down the steps towards the murderous cunts.

I was probably few hundred yards from them, people had started abandoning the crowd, trampling over one another, doing horrific things just to try and save their own backs but to no avail.

Then one of the bastards turned on me.

I dropped to the floor but not before I felt something whack against my arm just above the elbow. I had been shot. It fucking hurt. I rolled across the littered ground, dead and injured people everywhere.

One of the soldiers had taken the opportunity to attack the gunman whilst his attention was on me. I cheered as I saw the guy thrust his bayonet straight through the bastard's back and saw the tip burst from his chest. The soldier pushed the gunman to the ground and was instantly decapitated by the remaining one's fire.

I picked up the gun and ran towards the last gunman.

He was being more careful with his shots, taking out all the soldiers until none were left.

I could hear and see the armies of police approaching the entrance but wondered how many more people would be slain before the gunman was either taken down or turned the gun on himself. The fucker started on the row of pipers who stood steadfast until the bullets tore them apart, the defiant warriors refusing to buckle and surrender to their enemy. Scotland the brave, man. The gunman stopped to reload. I sped up, seizing the moment. All that was remained were those who wondered how many more bullets the man had left and whether it would be them or a loved one who would be taken. Standing above the frightened crowd, the lone piper. The one from my fucking dreams. As I got closer I saw the poor fella was in a right state, badly burnt and barely standing but something in the poor bastard made him want to play his pipes until they inflated with his last breath and sung the notes of his dying.

"Scotland the brave!" I screamed in a war cry as I ran towards the last gunman. This is it, I thought as he turned his weapon on me but his gun got stuck. I ploughed into him and as we went down his gun went off and the piper stopped, the bagpipes giving one last pathetic wheeze. "No!" I cried and looked down at the laughing muttering bastard. He didn't care, he expected to die, was all part of the cunt's bigger plan, whether it be a deluded promise to some Creator, or just some brainwashed cult. There was no fear in the fucker's eyes at all. I was going to kill the bastard so fucking much.

I raised the hard butt of the gun above his head, his face covered in blood spatter and perspiration, smiling, nodding.

I used the weapon to pound the living shit out of the fucker's arms until they were nothing but rags on the dirt. I dragged the cunt by the ankles across the Esplanade, screaming, "Scotland the brave!" I think I had gone a wee bit nuts by then. People looked at me like I was a hero or something, I didn't feel like one. I passed the lone piper, bullet wound in his left eye just like in my dream, and dragged the fucker towards the approaching police and medical crews. As we met I could hear the chanting of the people behind me spur me on even though the blood coming out of my arm was making me giddy.

Scotland the brave.

Scotland the brave.

Scotland the brave.

Author Biographies

Em Dehaney

Em Dehaney is a mother of two, a writer of fantasy and a drinker of tea. Born in Gravesend, England, her writing is inspired by the dark and decadent history of her home town. She is made of tea, cake, blood and magic.

Her poem 'Here We Come A-Wassailing' was originally in the Burdizzo Books 12Days Christmas anthology. This was her first published work and put her in touch with Matthew Cash, the creator of Burdizzo Books. They formed an unholy partnership, and together released The Reverend Burdizzo's Hymn Book, which marked Em's first foray into editing and contains her short story "For Those In Peril On The Sea".

Her collection of short stories and poetry, 'Food of The Gods', is available now on Amazon.

Her main literary influences are Stephen King, Neil Gaiman, Graham Masterton and Poppy Z Brite, and while her published works to date have been mainly horror, Em writes anything that takes her fancy and doesn't like to be pinned down to one genre. Her debut novel, The Golden Virginian, is an urban fantasy which draws heavily on local history and is due for release soon. A lifelong music lover, Em will listen to everything from acid house to experimental jazz, but her musical inspiration tends to come from Bjork, Fiona Apple, Regina Spektor, PJ Harvey and Super Furry Animals. Her obsessions include reading about Jack The Ripper, Reeses Peanut Butter Cups and smashing the patriarchy.

By night Em is The Black Nun, editor and whip-cracker at Burdizzo Books.

By day you can always find her at

http://www.emdehaney.com/

or lurking about on Facebook

https://www.facebook.com/emdehaney/

posting pictures of witches.

She also twitters about things at @emdehaney

Krzysztof Wroński

Krzysztof Wroński lives in the Polish city of Gdynia. He's a 30 y.o. illustrator, a busy musician, a dreadful stories writer, and a big fan of weird-fiction and horror stories. But generally speaking: he's a freelancing graphic artist who prefers to draw on a paper more than on a computer. Mostly, he works with dip pens and a black ink, despite the fact that it's easier to make a mistake and harder to fix it.

He has started drawing with a university course. He's an archaeologist and thought that would need an experience in 3D graphic for his further studies but it didn't. But when he was on a graphic course he realized what he's always wanted to do. Drawing and designing graphics. Now he's finishing his PhD in history on University of Gdańsk but looking for a job that gives him true happiness which is graphic design.

Most of his work is done with nib and ink, referring to the traditions of former masters such as Albrecht Dürer, Martin Schongauer, Urs Graf, Theodor Kittelsen, Hieronymus Bosch and Harry Clarke. This is a very laborious way of illustrating, but it is characterized by great detail and originality. In his private projects he is inspired by the themes of Pomerania's old history and Pomeranian folklore, a mixture of Polish, Kashubian and German influences. He often plays upon my love of horror films and weird fiction literature to bring the viewer to a new way of looking at an ordinary scene.

Links:

Web: www.wronski-artwork.pl

Instagram: @krzysztofwronski

Facebook: @wronski.art.work

Matthew Cash

Matthew Cash, or Matty-Bob Cash as he is known to most, was born and raised in Suffolk; which is the setting for his debut novel Pinprick. He is compiler and editor of Death By Chocolate, a chocoholic horror Anthology, the 12Days: STOCKING FILLERS Anthology, SPARKS: an electrical horror anthology*, The Reverend Burdizzo's Hymn Book*, Under The Weather** and has numerous releases on Kindle and several collections in paperback.

In 2016 he started his own label Burdizzo Books, with the intention of compiling and releasing charity anthologies a few times a year. He is currently working on numerous projects, his third novel FUR was launched in 2018.

* With Em Dehaney
**With Em Dehaney & Back Road Books

He has always written stories since he first learnt to write and most, although not all, tend to slip into the many layered murky depths of the Horror genre.

His influences ranged from when he first started reading to Present day are, to name but a small select few; Roald Dahl, James Herbert, Clive Barker, Stephen King, Stephen Laws, and more recently he enjoys Adam Nevill, F.R Tallis, Michael Bray, Gary Fry, William Meikle and Iain Rob Wright (who featured Matty-Bob in his famous A-Z of Horror title M is For Matty-Bob, plus Matthew wrote his own version of events which was included as a bonus).

He is a father of two, a husband of one and a zoo keeper of numerous fur babies.

You can find him here:
www.facebook.com/pinprickbymatthewcash
https://www.amazon.co.uk/-/e/B010MQTWKK

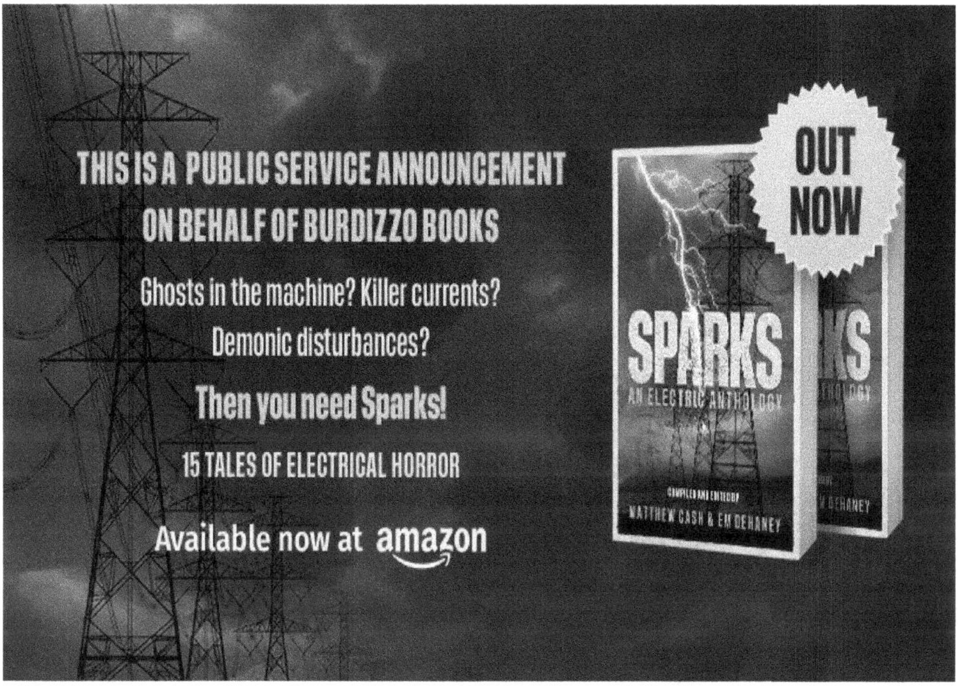
THIS IS A PUBLIC SERVICE ANNOUNCEMENT
ON BEHALF OF BURDIZZO BOOKS
Ghosts in the machine? Killer currents?
Demonic disturbances?
Then you need Sparks!
15 TALES OF ELECTRICAL HORROR
Available now at amazon
OUT NOW
SPARKS
AN ELECTRIC ANTHOLOGY
COMPILED AND EDITED BY
MATTHEW CASH & EM DEHANEY

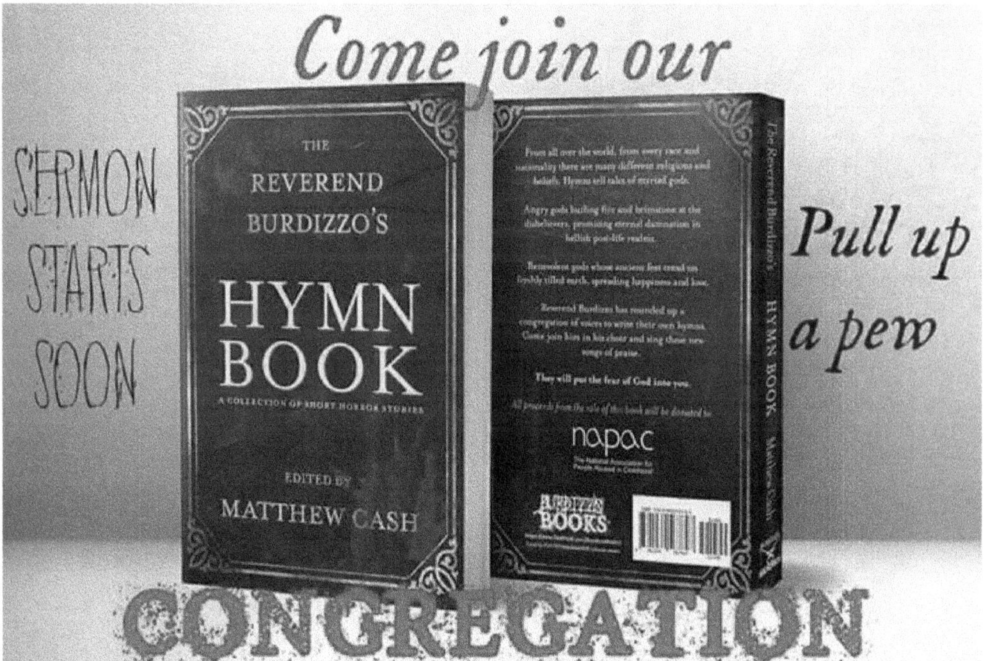
Come join our
SERMON STARTS SOON
THE REVEREND BURDIZZO'S
HYMN BOOK
A COLLECTION OF SHORT HORROR STORIES
EDITED BY
MATTHEW CASH
They will put the fear of God into you.
napac
BURDIZZO BOOKS
Pull up a pew
CONGREGATION

IT'S CHRISTMAS TIME, THERE'S NO NEED
TO BE AFRAID...
ALL PROCEEDS GO TO
Cystic Fibrosis Trus
12 DAYS
MATTHEW CASH
12 DAYS
MATTHEW CASH
12 DAYS
Available at
amazon

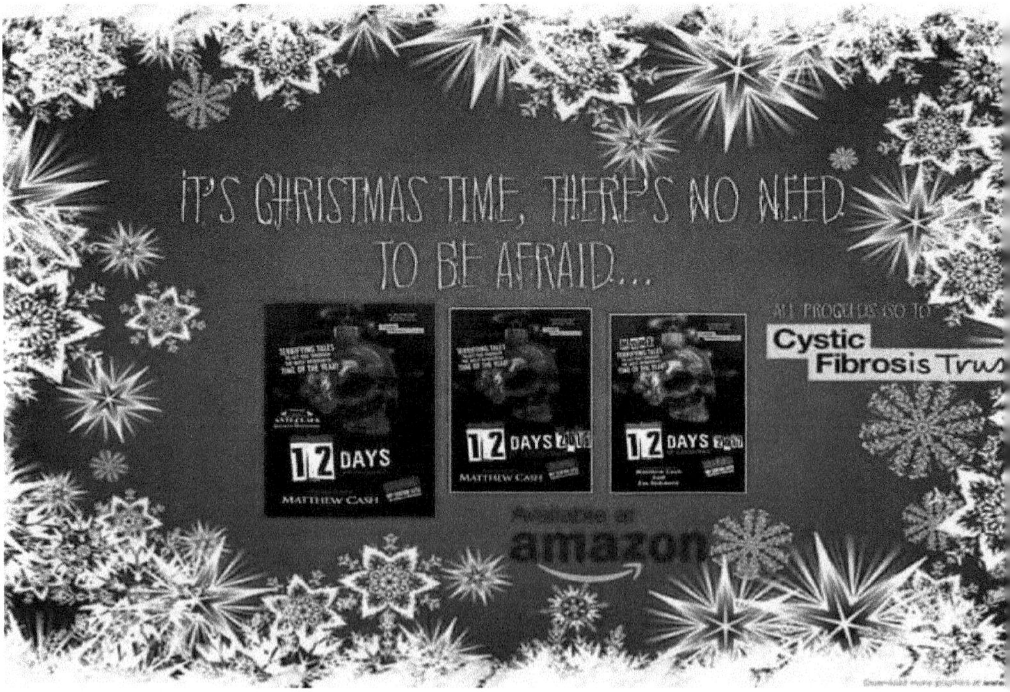

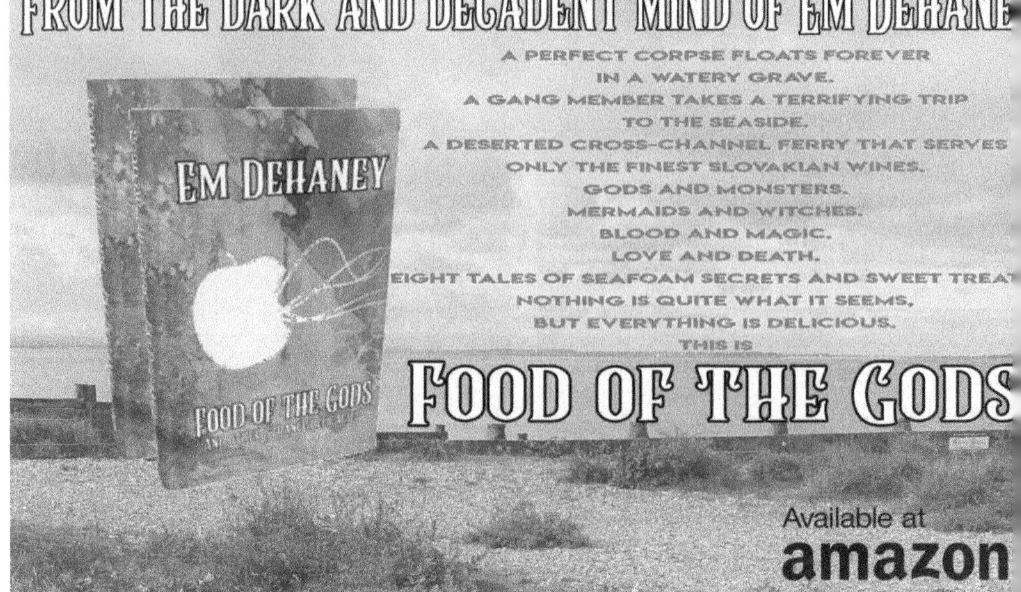

FROM THE DARK AND DECADENT MIND OF EM DEHANE
A PERFECT CORPSE FLOATS FOREVER
IN A WATERY GRAVE.
A GANG MEMBER TAKES A TERRIFYING TRIP
TO THE SEASIDE.
A DESERTED CROSS-CHANNEL FERRY THAT SERVES
ONLY THE FINEST SLOVAKIAN WINES.
GODS AND MONSTERS.
MERMAIDS AND WITCHES.
BLOOD AND MAGIC.
LOVE AND DEATH.
EIGHT TALES OF SEAFOAM SECRETS AND SWEET TREA
NOTHING IS QUITE WHAT IT SEEMS,
BUT EVERYTHING IS DELICIOUS.
THIS IS
FOOD OF THE GODS
EM DEHANEY
FOOD OF THE GODS
Available at
amazon

www.ingramcontent.com/pod-product-compliance
Ingram Content Group UK Ltd.
Pitfield, Milton Keynes, MK11 3LW, UK
UKHW021432280726
14060UKWH00001BA/30